Emma

The Incredible story of

Dennis

the cavity

Chapter One

Josh was eight years old, and like many other boys his age, he had his own set of rules that he lived by. These rules, well they were less like rules and more like standards of living. He did not like to take a bath unless he had too, he hated combing his hair, and he only brushed his teeth when his mom made him. And flossing? You could forget flossing; that was not ever going to happen.

He was an only child and he lived with his mom and dad in a house in a small town. His parents both had to work, so he spent his afternoons at his grandmother's house. She let him watch TV, sit on a big soft couch and play video games for as long as he wanted to. Best of all, she always made sure he had cookies, candy, and soda. He could eat whatever he wanted, and she never told him no, like his mom did.

His mom was always worried about something; Josh thought she was too worried about a lot of stuff that never happened. She worried that he would catch cold if he didn't wear a hat, that never happened. She was worried he would strain his eyes if he sat too close to the TV, he could see just fine, thank you. And she was worried he ate too much sugar, which he would get cavities. So far, he did not have any cavities; he was not real sure what a cavity was, but he didn't have any, he thought.

Every day after school, Josh went to his grandmother's house. He sat on her couch, and he played his Xbox One or his PS4. Every day, the conversation went something like this.

"Josh, how was school?" his grandmother would ask with a smile.

"It was good, grandma." He would say as he dropped his book bag on the floor and turned on his game system.

"That's nice, do you have any homework?" she would ask him.

"No, I did it at school" He would lie. He almost always had homework, but he would do it when he got home after dinner. He did not want to lose the chance anytime he could be spending playing his favorite games.

"Okay Josh, I baked you some cookies today. They're your favorite, chocolate chip." She would say as she brought him a whole plate of cookies.

"Thanks, grandma, can I have some chocolate milk?" he would ask as he ate his cookies.

"You sure can." She would say and bring him a big, tall glass of chocolate milk.

Every day after school. He would gulp down the milk with the cookies, cake, or candy she was always making for him. He would then have at least 1 glass or sometimes 2 glasses of soda pop. He loved candy, cakes, chocolate milk and soda pop. He loved sugar and would eat it every day. He believed it made him a better gamer.

It was a Friday afternoon like any other Friday to Josh. He sat on the couch playing his sports game and drinking soda pop. He was unaware that this Wednesday was different, even though he did not know it, yet.

The last time Josh had brushed his teeth was early that morning. Since then, he had two glasses of chocolate milk at lunch, and after school, he had eaten waffles with lots of syrup, a candy bar, a peanut butter and jelly sandwich, 4 homemade oatmeal cookies, and rank a glass of soda pop. He had spent the whole day eating sugar, sugar, and more sugar. Deep in his mouth, unknown to him, something was happening, something bad.

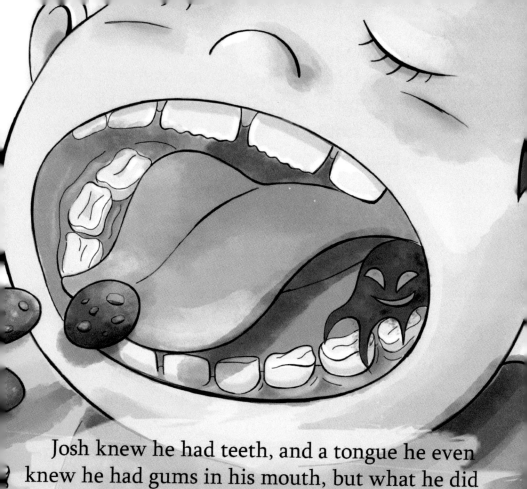

Josh knew he had teeth, and a tongue he even knew he had gums in his mouth, but what he did not know was that there was something else in his mouth, something scary, it was called dental caries. Caries is a weird name for something that everyone knows all too well as cavities.

A cavity is a word you don't want to hear when you are sitting at a dentist's office. It is the breakdown and decay of a tooth, and it is caused by bacteria. At that very moment, on a Wednesday afternoon while Josh played the latest football video game, dental caries named Dennis was waking up from a long sleep.

It had been two months since Josh's last check up at the dentist. Doctor Johnson had warned him to be careful about the sugar he was eating. His teeth cleaning had not gone well, and the dentist was worried that he would start to get cavities if he did not change his ways. Dennis the dental caries had been hiding out in the back of Josh's mouth just waiting for the cleaning to be over. He had chuckled that the dentist had missed him once again and that he would be back to try to take over Josh's mouth one tooth at a time, one day in the very near future.

Well, that day was now. Dennis crawled out from behind a big tooth called a molar on the left side of Josh's mouth. He had been sleeping in the gooey plaque that was building up just under the gum line. The plaque was made of up of acid and tiny particles of food. It was so smelly and sticky, and he loved it.

He had woke up that afternoon covered in sticky sugar from head to toe. When he crawled out from behind the molar, he was delighted by what he saw. He looked up into Josh's mouth and saw sugar, and the plaque was covering every surface. He even noticed that some of the plaque looked like it had been there since right after the last dental cleaning.

He smiled a toothy grin as Josh took a big gulp

of sugary soda pop. The dark sticky liquid rushed past Dennis, slid down Josh's tongue and down his throat. He looked around the mouth and saw that all of Josh's teeth were shiny with the left-over soda that coated each and every one. It was a beautiful sight, he thought. He was ready to begin his evil plan to take over Josh's mouth once and for all.

Chapter Two

Dennis knew that there was no better time than now to begin an attack on Josh's mouth. He was strong by himself, but he knew he would need help. He could not take over Josh's mouth all alone. He thought about how he was going to attack the teeth in Josh's mouth, and the answer came to him in a flash, just like lightening. He would get the help he needed from the scary bacteria monsters also known as Streptococcus mutans. These bacteria monsters were his closest friends. They were very small, yet they were very dangerous when a lot of them got together.

These bacteria did not need to be big to do a lot of damage. Like a bad guy in a comic book, these bacteria seemed normal on the outside, but they had a secret super power that made them monsters. They could take all the sugar that was laying around Josh's mouth and coated in his teeth and turn sugar into acid. That acid was lactic acid, and it could do really bad things to Josh' teeth. These bacteria could corrode the teeth and then go on to form plaque. These bacteria were so powerful that they were the only ones that could form receptors that made it easy to stick to Josh's teeth.

Dennis was not only relying on the help of Streptococcus mutans, but also Lactobacillus. This bacterium was rod shaped. Depending on the species, it could be used for good things such as making yogurt, cheese, and pickles, but left in Josh's mouth it was a real monster. It could corrode teeth and lead to tooth decay.

Dennis was glad to have the two bacteria working side by side with him on this project. Each different kind of bacteria was a band and capable of doing damage to Josh's teeth, but together they were even more scary. Together they could produce a super weapon called a biofilm. Both bacteria had to be together to transfer enough of their genes to each other to create the dreaded biofilm.

Dennis knew that the word biofilm was just a fancy way of saying plaque. Plaque stuck to the teeth can cause a rapid increase in decay and

damage. He called his friends together to tell them about his evil plan.

Dennis looked at Josh's mouth and was pleased that he already saw a nice thick coating of plaque on his teeth. He called his friends together to tell them about his evil plan.

"Bacteria in Dennis's mouth, it is good to see you on this fine Wednesday afternoon."

The bacteria gathered at the gum line and all cheered and clapped. They were so small that Josh could not hear them or feel them, but they were there.

"Raise your hands in the air if you are here to do some damage?"

Everyone raised their hands.

"Good, who here wants to cause decay and de-struction, who wants to turn Josh's white teeth into teeth that are black and brown? Who is with me as we cause big holes in his teeth called cavi-ties?"

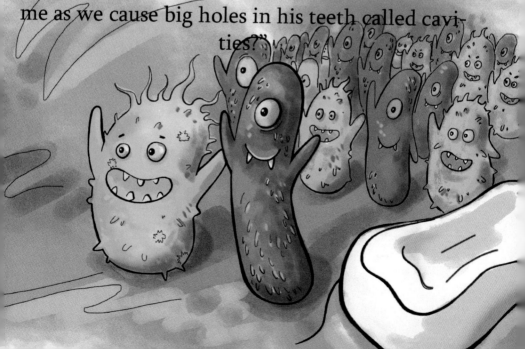

The crowd of bacteria went wild. They were extremely happy to be part of such an important mission. It was not often that a single bacterium had a real chance to make a difference, but none of the bacteria were by themselves, there were thousands of them all together. Dennis knew looking out over the crowd that together all of them could wipe out all the teeth in Josh's mouth if they really wanted to.

"I have a plan for how we are going to make a mess of Josh's teeth. This is how we are going to do it. First Josh is already helping us out with this one, he's not brushing, and he never flosses. It's like he wants to get tooth decay." He said as a joke.

The bacteria in the audience laughed and giggled.

"Second, all this sugar that you see laying around and sticky food particles that are rich in

sucrose, we are going to convert that sugar into the lactic acid.

This will lead to tooth decay. When that phase is done, we are going to work together and create the best biofilm that has ever existed in Josh's mouth." He said

He walked over to an old friend a bacterium named Harvey, he shook his hand up and asked him what he wanted to see, Harvey smiled and said "Tooth decay!"

Dennis laughed at the thought while the bacteria started jumping up and down in excitement. He said, "I want to create a plaque that is so sticky and so full of bacteria that will not only take over one or two teeth but maybe even all the teeth in the back, top and bottom of his mouth."

Dennis climbed a molar and looked out over the crowd of bacteria they were cheering and clap-ping.

Some of them were so happy that they were danc-
ing! He held up his hands to quiet the crowd., he
finished his speech, "When I look around Josh's
mouth I see healthy white teeth, I am disgusted by
such a sight, I want to see teeth that are full of
cavities. I want to see bleeding gums, and I want
to see teeth getting pulled in the future. I want his
mouth to look like we have been here!"

He climbed back down and ordered his friends
to get to work. They had a lot of work to do, and
they needed to get started if they were going to
reach their goal. The first step was already under
way. Josh was not good at dental hygiene, so they
had everything that they needed to be successful.
They had sugar, plaque, no flossing and a steady
diet of sugar and carbohydrates like cakes and
cookies. Dennis could not have asked for a better
place to create a paradise of cavities and tooth
decay.

Chapter Three

Now that all the sugar was in place and Josh showed no signs of changing his ways, it was time to begin the attack. Dennis led the charge of the bacteria monsters. They waded in a sea of sticky sugar, soda residue and plaque until they could reach the back teeth Dennis wanted to attack the back teeth first. Dennis had been in Josh's mouth for a long time, and he knew all about his bad tooth brushing habits.

Josh rarely brushed his teeth, and when he did, he never paid any attention to brushing his teeth the way he was supposed to. He brushed the front ones and sometimes forgot all about the back ones. Dennis knew that the back teeth were dirty and covered with more sugar than the front. Since he never flossed, Dennis was sure that Josh would never do anything that might put a stop to their evil plan.

The bacteria monsters all rushed the back teeth. They approached the teeth and surrounded them. They waded in sticky sugar and plaque up to their knees. The attached themselves to the teeth with their special receptors. Now it would be very hard to get them off Josh's teeth.

Now that they were attached to the back teeth, the bacteria monsters started gobbling up the sugar at an alarming rate. They sucked up as much sugar left over from all the cookies, candy, cakes, chocolate milk and soda pop. It was old and rotting, so it smelled bad and tasted as it smelled to anyone else but these bacteria monsters, they loved it. Rotting sugar particles and soda pop were on of their favorite foods.

They ate the sugar and licked the soda pop. With their super power, they turned all the sugar they ate into lactic acid. They spread this acid all over the teeth and waited patiently. Lactic acid was the secret ingredient in a process known as demineralization.

What Josh did not know, and what Dennis and his bacteria friends did was how a tooth stays strong and what makes them weak. Teeth are made of minerals that are always changing. These minerals in the top layer of the tooth called the enamel, are getting lost and then replaced on a daily basis.

Josh could not feel it or see it, but it was happening. The bacteria monsters had spread lactic acid all over the teeth which meant that these teeth would not be able to replace the minerals that they had lost as fast as they needed to. These areas were softer than the rest of the tooth. The soft areas could now be attacked and destroyed. The bacteria monsters waited and waited. They kept eating sugar and spreading the lactic acid in the teeth. Finally, a few days later they noticed a good sign for them and a bad sign for Josh. They saw small chalky white spots appearing on the surface of the teeth they had coated with Lactic acid. These chalky white spots were the beginning of cavities It was a great day for the bacteria, it meant all their hard work was paying off. Dennis looked at the damage and was pleased with their hard work; everything was going according to plan. He gave the order to keep going, and his friends did just that, they kept going. They kept attacking the enamel and this time they brought out their secret weapon, the biofilm known as plaque. He called on both his friends the bacteria monsters known as Streptococcus mutans and Lactobacillus. They worked together and formed a plaque so heavy and thick that it would totally cover every part of the back teeth. The bacteria monsters shook hands and started creating the plaque right away.

It did not take long for the plaque to form. With the thick plaque in place, they could make a bigger attack against the enamel. This plaque was the perfect place for his bacteria monsters to reside and feed on sugar, causing the decay process to speed up. He gave the order and the bacteria monsters ate more sugar at an even faster rate of speed.

It was a couple of weeks later, that the Dennis saw 3 small black holes forming in the molars in Josh's mouth. They were tiny, but they were perceptible cavities. Josh had not noticed them yet; that was clear form his diet. He had not changed his ways; He was still eating cakey, sugary treats and drinking soda pop. These carbohydrates were just what the bacteria monsters needed to eat to get ready for the next phase.

Dennis breathed a sigh of relief, if Josh had taken better care of his teeth, then the process that he had started in Josh's mouth could have been reversed. Tooth decay is reversible at the first stage, the white chalky phase. He was glad Josh didn't know that as he watched a new shower of chocolate candy particles flood Josh s mouth. That candy would help his bacteria monster friends as they attacked the dentin.

Dennis knew that this part of his plan was going to be harder. He was glad that the bacteria monsters had all the sugar they could consume to help them.

He was emboldened by what he saw so far and knew that his plan was sure to succeed.

The bacteria monsters kept destroying the enamel until l one day they had a break through; they were through to the next layer of the tooth, the dentin. The dentin was not as easy to attack as the enamel, it fought back with a number of defenses. Josh's dentin could form different versions of itself to stop the invasion. The dentin tried to fight back by bringing immunoglobulins in to fight the infection. Unfortunately, there was a reaction which caused calcium and phosphorous to be released which weakened the dentin. No matter what it tried to do, the bacteria monsters were too strong.

Dennis was happy with his plan. Taking over Josh's mouth was going to be easier than he thought.

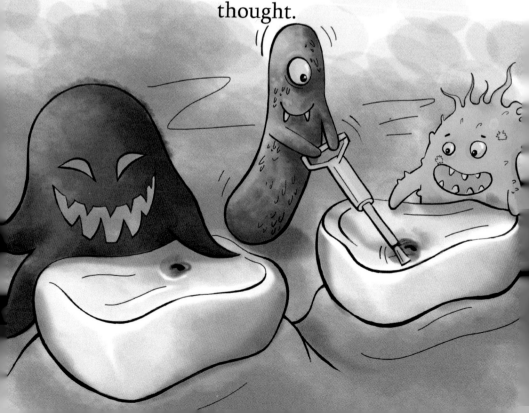

Chapter Four

Josh was eating candy and playing his PS4 when he noticed that a couple of his teeth hurt. He had noticed it a week ago when he was eating ice cream at Timothy's birthday party. The cold ice cream made his teeth hurt. He had never had anything like this happen before. He told his mom when he got home that night.

"Josh, I am not surprised your teeth hurt, I know you eat sugar all the time and you should do a better job brushing your teeth, I am going to call Doctor Johnson and make an appointment."

Josh hated going to the dentist, but now he had no choice. He was hurting, and his mom was making him go. The next morning, his mom called his school, then took him to the dentist. He sat in the dentist chair and listened as Doctor Johnson spoke to his mom.

"I see 3 cavities that need to be filled and a lot of plaque. If Josh doesn't change his ways he is going to have cavities so bad he may lose his teeth."

"Doctor Jonson, what can we do?" asked his mom.

"Be sure that he flosses every day and does a better job brushing his teeth. I would cut back the sugar, too."

Josh sat in the chair and tried to think of anything else while the dentist filled his cavities. He hated every second of it.

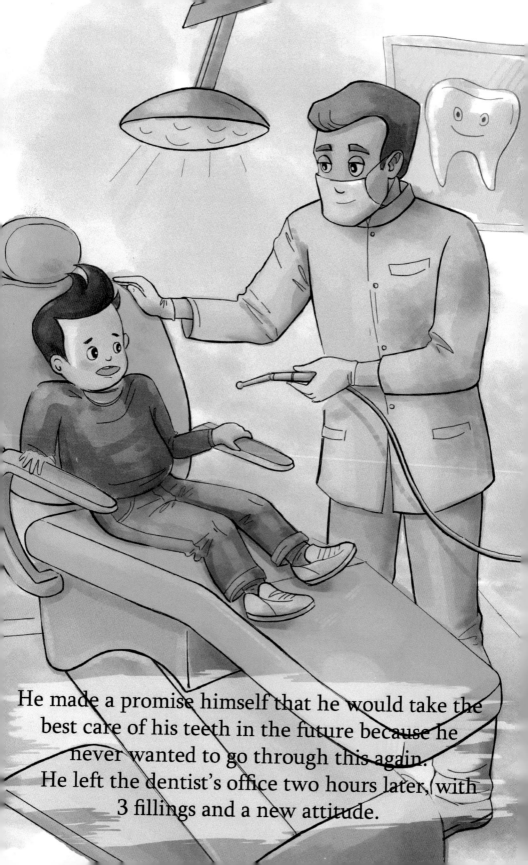

He made a promise himself that he would take the best care of his teeth in the future because he never wanted to go through this again.
He left the dentist's office two hours later, with 3 fillings and a new attitude.

That sweet night, before went to bed, he flossed his teeth. The dentist had shown him how and he intended to be the best flosser he could be.

Meanwhile, in his mouth, Dennis was disappointed, he had led his bacteria monsters to create 3 cavities, and now they had been filled. He would have to start over. All he had to do was only wait for a few weeks, and then he could begin a new attack, or so he thought.

He had to jump out of the way to avoid the floss and then hide really good to stay away from the toothpaste and the brush. What happened? He wondered as he hid. Had Josh changed his ways? He tried not to think about that. If that were true, then he would never have a chance to take over Josh's mouth, and that made him very unhappy.

Josh was done flossing and brushing, he looked in the mirror and smiled. His teeth were white, healthy and strong. He made the decision that he would change one of his rules; he would start flossing every day and brushing. His mom was right to worry about his teeth, and he thought he may even start wearing a hat just in case.

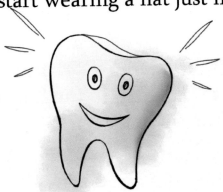

If you enjoyed this book, don't forget to leave a review on Amazon! I highly appreciate your reviews, and it only takes a minute to do.

Your Free Gift
I wanted to show my appreciation that you support my work so I've put together a free gift for you.
http://www.olkha.co/children-book-free.html
Just visit the link above to download it now.
I know child will love this gift.
Thanks!

Copyright 2017 by Emma Gertony - All rights reserved.

All rights Reserved. No part of this publication or the information in it may be quoted from or reproduced in any form by means such as printing, scanning, photocopying or otherwise without prior written permission of the copyright holder. Disclaimer and Terms of Use: Effort has been made to ensure that the information in this book is accurate and complete, however, the author and the publisher do not warrant the accuracy of the information, text and graphics contained within the book due to the rapidly changing nature of science, research, known and unknown facts and internet. The Author and the publisher do not hold any responsibility for errors, omissions or contrary interpretation of the subject matter herein. This book is presented solely for motivational and informational purposes only.

69278590R00018

Made in the USA
Middletown, DE
19 September 2019